*For God, who gave me Mendel,*
*For my parents, who gave me Holy Days,*
*For Charlie, who gives me miracles every day.*
M.A.

*To my mother.*
H.B.

Alborghetti, Marci.
Miracle of the myrrh / written by Marci Alborghetti ; illustrated by Hervé Blondon.
First Edition
p.   cm.
Summary: When Mary gives Mendel, a young handicapped boy, the gifts presented to the baby Jesus from the three wise men,
Mendel distributes them to those in need and receives a miracle in return.
ISBN: 1-890817-16-3
[1. Generosity-Fiction. 2. Jesus Christ-Fiction. 3. Physically Handicapped-Fiction. 4. Miracles-Fiction.]
I. Blondon, Hervé, ill. II. Title.
PZ7.A3227 Mi            2000
[E]—dc21
00-020551      CIP

Library of Congress catalog card number: 00-020551
Creative Director: Bretton Clark
Designed by Billy Kelly
Calligraphy by John Stevens
Editor: Margey Cuyler
Printed in Belgium

This book has a trade reinforced binding.

For games, links and more, visit our interactive Web site:

*winslowpress.com*

# The Miracle of the Myrrh

written by Marci Alborghetti

illustrated by Hervé Blondon

WINSLOW PRESS

DELRAY BEACH, FLORIDA • NEW YORK

After Grampa and the children had set up the crèche, the children gathered at their grandfather's knee.

"Grampa, what ever happened to the three gifts the Wise Men brought to the baby Jesus?" they asked. "We never hear about that."

"It's a wonderful story that goes back to the little drummer boy who led the Three Wise Men to Mary, Joseph, and the baby Jesus," said Grampa. "Mary and Joseph could see that the drummer boy would make a perfect big brother for Jesus, so they adopted him and named him Simon."

"Did he always live with Jesus?"

"They grew up together, and were as close as two brothers could be. Then, Simon got married and had a little son named Mendel. When Jesus became a traveling preacher, Simon followed him."

"Did Mendel go with his father and Jesus also?"

"No, because even though Mendel's heart was filled with goodness, he was born with paralyzed legs. He couldn't walk or run like other children. But he never complained. In fact, Jesus made Mendel a little cart that the boy wheeled around the neighborhood. Sometimes Mendel wheeled over to help Mary, Jesus' Mother, with her chores. Mary showed Mendel the gifts of gold, frankincense, and myrrh that the Wise Men had brought to Jesus so many years before."

"So tell us now about what happened to the gifts."

"All right. Come closer, and you'll hear about a miracle that happened nearly 2,000 years ago. . . ."

Every morning, Simon pushed Mendel in his little cart along the rough, rutted path to Mary's hut. It was tucked into the bottom of a hill and shaded by a grove of fig trees. Mendel liked to help Mary bake bread for the poor of Jerusalem in the one room where she slept, cooked, and ate her meals.

One morning, Mary was waiting for Simon and Mendel by her door. "Come in," she said. "I want to tell you both something important."

Simon and Mendel went inside and settled at the table. "Soon, I will leave this world to join my Son, Jesus," said Mary. "Before I go, I have something special to give Mendel."

She reached up to a shelf and took down a package wrapped in brown cloth. It contained three colored sacks. Mary opened the sack that was as green as moss and poured out a pile of shimmering gold. Next, she opened the sack that was as red as pomegranates and lifted out a vial of frankincense with a scent sweeter than lilies. The third sack, bluer than the sea, held a small, heavy jar filled with myrrh.

As Mary placed each gift before Mendel, she explained: "When the Three Wise Men visited Jesus in His manger, they brought gifts of gold, frankincense, and myrrh. I saved those treasures, hoping that Jesus might use them for His own family some day. But this was not God's plan for Jesus. Now, I wish to give them to another child I love. They are yours, Mendel. Use them wisely."

Many feelings rushed through Mendel. He was surprised and honored and even a little afraid because he knew what a responsibility Mary was giving him. He hoped he would have the wisdom to use the gifts well.

Simon leaned forward, a frown lining his face. "We cannot accept the gifts that belonged to Jesus. It would not be right."

Mary answered gently, "This is God's will for Mendel." And so Simon agreed.

Mendel and Simon returned home and showed the treasures to Salome.

"At last, we have some luck!" she exclaimed. "We can use the gold to buy medicine for Mendel. There will be plenty left to purchase fabric so I can make new clothes to replace the rags we wear now. Quick, give me the gold so I can run to the city marketplace."

"Please, Mother!" cried Mendel. "We cannot use these gifts. I must give them to others with greater needs."

"What are you saying?" shouted Salome. "My hands are as raw and red as these cheap clay bowls from years of washing, cleaning, and cooking! While your father deserted us to follow Jesus, I exhausted myself with work and worry. And now, when I finally have a chance to relax and enjoy life, you snatch that hope away to give to others. Ungrateful child!"

With that, Salome stormed from their hut. Mendel hated to see his mother in such a state, but he knew the gifts were not meant for selfish use.

The next morning, Mendel heard a noisy crowd in the street. When he wheeled his cart outside, he found the neighbors gathered around the well, chattering with news that Mary was gone. Some claimed to have seen her rise above their huts in a bright cloud. Others said an angel came to her door and took her away.

Only Mendel knew what had really happened. He had dreamed that Mary had come to his little cot and had placed her cool, soft hand on his cheek. Smiling, she had whispered, "Good-bye, my little helper." Then, she had risen into Heaven.

Mendel believed the dream. As he lay under his rough blanket holding the gifts that Mary had given him, he promised himself he would use the treasures wisely.

The next day, Simon brought bad news to Salome and Mendel. Their neighbor, Matthius, had been beaten by some soldiers who stole his flock of sheep. "When Matthius tried to stop them," Simon told them, "they struck and ridiculed him, saying that he should ask Jesus to rise again and give him new sheep."

"See?" cried Salome bitterly. "Following Jesus and Mary didn't do Matthius any good!"

Simon ignored her outburst and said, "Mendel and I will go to Matthius and offer him help." Mendel barely had time to grab the green sack from its hiding place under his blanket before Simon lifted him to his shoulders and trudged out the door.

Although Matthius was badly beaten, he rose shakily to welcome them.

Simon said, "We have come to help you, my friend."

"Thank you," answered the shepherd, "but you can do nothing. A new flock costs too much. My family must work for the merchants at the bazaar, and even then, it will take us many years to save enough for new sheep."

"Do not worry," said Mendel. He removed the green sack from inside his robe and handed it to Matthius. "Mary gave me this gold. Since the shepherds were the first to visit the baby Jesus, it is right for you to take this gift and buy a flock as soon as you can. Please accept it."

Matthius's hand trembled as he reached for the gold. "Thank you," he whispered, falling to his knees. Simon and Mendel went out into the cool night, leaving Matthius and his family singing praises to God.

News of Mendel's generosity spread fast. By the time Mendel and Simon reached home, Salome knew of her son's gift to Matthius. She shouted at Simon, "How could you let him give away all that gold when we need it so badly?"

Simon answered, "Our son has done well, Salome. We should be proud."

Salome shook her head but said no more.

The next morning, a neighbor rushed into their home, saying, "The high priest turned old Anna out of the temple. She has been taken to the home of her husband's relations, but she just lies there on her bed, crying for Mary."

Mendel remembered Mary telling him about Anna's faith in Jesus and God, His Father. The old woman had spent all her days in the temple, praising God and calling out that Jesus was the Savior, the Messiah of Israel. Mary had protected Anna, rubbing healing oils into her old and aching muscles when she grew tired. Now, Mary was gone, and there was no one to care for her.

Mendel told Simon, "Father, we must go to Anna. She needs our help." And while Salome was busy hanging their wash out to dry, Mendel wheeled to his cot and grasped the red sack.

Simon lifted Mendel and carried him to the place where Anna rested. She lay on a pallet, her skin wrinkled and dry like crumpled vines, her eyes closed. Simon gently placed Mendel by her side. Mendel put the slender vial of frankincense in her gnarled hand, saying, "This gift comes from Mary. You can use it to worship God wherever you are."

Anna's eyes brightened when Mendel opened the flask and the beautiful fragrance of frankincense filled the room. "This incense will carry my prayers to Heaven," she said. Filled with new hope, she arose from the pallet, singing prayers and lighting the holy oil.

Salome was waiting when they returned home. Again, word had reached her about Mendel's gift to Anna. Before she could even complain, Mendel took her chapped hand in his, saying, "Do not worry, Mother. God will reward you in Heaven if you share the riches in your home and your heart here on Earth."

Salome saw light in Mendel's eyes. She grew silent, thinking about her son's words as she prepared dinner.

Mendel went to bed right after supper but he tossed and turned, twisting his coarse blanket in his hands. He was worried. Tomorrow was Jesus' birthday, and Mendel still hadn't found a way to give the third gift. He thought if he went to Mary's hut to pray, he might have an idea.

Early the next morning, Mendel took the blue sack of myrrh and asked his father to wheel him to Mary's deserted home. When they arrived, Simon kissed his young son and left. Mendel prayed through the morning and the afternoon, thinking, If I keep asking God and Mary for a sign, I know they'll help me.

Nighttime approached. Mendel's face became as long as the shadows in Mary's cold hut. No message had come from Heaven, and Mendel knew his parents would worry if he missed dinner. He lifted the blue sack, thinking, I'll take one last look inside and maybe then I'll see the sign I've been missing.

But the soft blue silk slipped through his fingers, and the jar of precious myrrh fell to the floor and shattered! A smell of roses filled the room as the precious ointment sprayed all over the cart and Mendel's thin little legs!

"What have I done?" cried Mendel. "I've been clumsy and ruined the third gift!" Sad and exhausted, Mendel knew he should go home before Simon came searching for him. Sobbing, he turned his cart toward the door.

As he wheeled onto the path, he felt a strange tingling in his legs. Then they began to tremble. He could feel his legs! He could feel his toes! He could even feel the myrrh smooth and wet on his skin. He began to wiggle each toe as his tears turned to joyful laughter.

Now Mendel understood why he had not known how to give the third gift. The myrrh was Mary's and Jesus' gift to him on Jesus' birthday.

Mendel jumped up and began running toward the hill near Mary's hut. He saw Simon in the distance, coming toward him. Mendel ran faster and threw himself into his father's arms. "Father!" he shouted. "I can walk! I can run! It's a miracle!"

Simon hugged his son tightly, tears soaking his face and beard as he said a prayer of thanks.

"I'll run ahead and surprise Mother," Mendel called. "Besides," he said, laughing, "you could never keep up with me now!"

When Simon got home, he found Salome sitting on the floor with Mendel in her lap. She stroked his hair with tears of joy shining in her eyes. Softly she told Mendel, "At last I know why your father loved Jesus, and why Mary loved you. My heart now rejoices in the gift Jesus has given you. This is the Miracle of the Myrrh."

Author's Note

*The Miracle of the Myrrh* is an original story about what might have happened to the little drummer boy, the subject of a well-known legend, and the three gifts of the Magi. Although Simon was a close friend and follower of Jesus, he is not to be confused with one of the Twelve Apostles. The story takes place in Jerusalem, where it is believed Mary stayed in the house of John the Apostle, "the one whom Jesus loved," after Christ died, rose, and ascended to Heaven. John was rarely at home since he traveled to faraway places, spreading the word of Christ. According to legend, Mary "fell asleep" and rose into Heaven while in Jerusalem. However, there are also Christians who believe that Mary died in Ephesus, where she might have lived with the apostle John in his later years.

Anna, the recipient of the gift of frankincense, is based on the old woman who first met Mary and Jesus when the young mother presented her baby in the temple to offer gifts of purification and thanksgiving after His birth. Anna was one of the early believers who declared that Jesus, although only a baby then, was the Messiah.